I0702372

"The stoicism of eating pussy in poetry comes by no surprise, or amateur tongue. Dane Ince's work of Licks & Drips on ice creamed slits fresco-fucks each page along a Frisco border." - Dane Ince's work reflectively rides into steamy sex scenes filling the holes of human separation. Pulp Poetry from San Francisco is a fist-fucking word pounding that'll make your lips bleed.

- Frogg Corpse Poet Vocalist Photographer Actor author of "The Mourning Hour Poetry to Die By "

"The hard-boiled steaming hot bloody sweaty sex and crime underworld Beat Noir poems of DESTINY MURDER get darker and faster moving down that long-distance railroad track to nowhere but man oh man they cast a spell so there's no way I'm gonna get off this night train! What a ride! Dane Ince is both Chief Detective and Public Enemy # 1. His poems mesmerize and summon me to the heart of darkness where the only choice is to do or die. DESTINY MURDER is a dangerous new volume of poems by the brilliant Dane Ince. I recommend it with only one warning: Get ready for the ride of your life! I hope you survive!"

- Ron Whitehead, Lifetime Beat Poet

It only takes a fraction of a moment, when you open the pages of Destiny Murder ! to know you are reading a true beat poet's book. From the opening line in the title piece " She folded my brain." To some of last words of the book "My brain unfolding the folds" nothing is wasted. The spaces filled as only Dane can do. Stories within stories.

- Fin Hall. Poet, filmmaker, publisher. New Pitsligo. Scotland

Destiny Murder read like a dramatic monolog for the stage...a great sense of time...character...place action..."flip a coin to bet myself...I win I lose again.." Or "It feels odd to speak of skies...there is only one sky..." Place: Pewter apartments painted tragically...the color bleeds upon gray sidewalk black" ...Metaphorical action: Nothing can fill me fuller than the savage attack of butterflies":" You need an ice pick to answer the phone. " I can hear a character for the stage saying this. Or " She opened me up like a killed rabbit and ripped out the guts of my soul...". or No one wants to hold a bag of smelly bones weeping." Just damn good writing.

Michael Lynch, Central Valley California, Award-winning Playwright in residence San Francisco One Act Theatre. MFA Northwestern University..Prof of Theatre Arts Modesto JC

Destiny Murder, pulled scratching and bleeding from California Beat Poet Laureate Dane Ince's heart snd soul, is an exhilarating, addictive walk on streets that are pitch black even at noon. Ignore the direction given in "Eternal." Instead, pick up these poems, pick up these tears. Ince's visions and their words will hold you over the fire. And then drop you in.

- Lennart Lundh: poet, photographer, historian, short-fictionist author of *Cutting a Sunbeam* Orland Hills, IL

In Dane Ince's new collection "Destiny Murder!", the poet challenges us to drop our costumes and come to this party fully nude and vulnerable. These poems hit on a nerve or loss over a breakup or beyond, and the poet not only releases themselves but the wonderful tensions explored throughout this manuscript.

- Thomas Fucaloro: author of The Only Gardening I do is When I Give Up by Finishing Line Press Staten Island,NY

Dane Ince shows consistency and brilliance with his new book "Destiny Murder!" Filling the eye and mind with images reflective of the great noir detective thrillers while not missing the subtleties. I particularly enjoy the sidesteps, such as the short piece "Cup" as the sensory aspect of a creative tale, like the devil, is in the details. Excellent work and much to be applauded. If Raymond Chandler and Lord Byron had a lovechild, here he is.

- William F. DeVault, US National Beat Poet Laureate Emeritus, Publisher Spider Press, author of "Eroica" Los Angeles

I admit to not being all that familiar with Beat poetry (or Noir for that matter) It appears that the protagonist is on a mission which culminates in his death. Meanwhile there is an exploration of the tragic and the senseless... And the internalisation ther-of. There is a recognition of societies failure (The King sent to prison? Trump?) "We failed to do our duty" (An irony of those servicemen who have rejected American foreign policy?) Everything is my favourite poem. ("Attack of butterflies"... Great line. Really... not a wasted word. Inspires so many 'pictures' in my mind. I could spend many hours 'talking' to these poems.

- Michael Gerard Collins New South Wales Australia

DESTINY MURDER!

Pulp Poems

BEAT NOIR

POETRY

By

DANE INCE

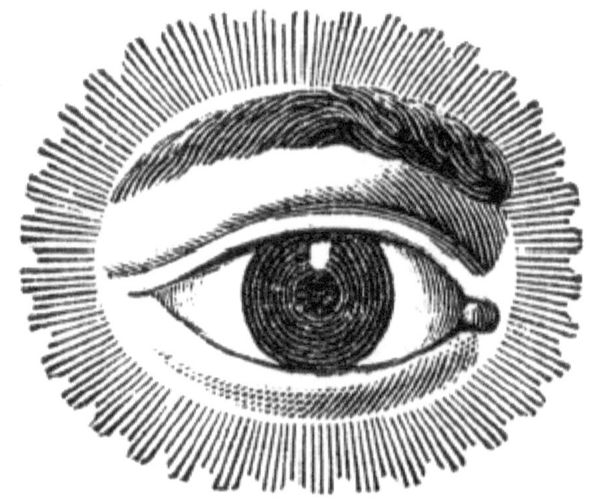

PUBLISH

EYEPUBLISHEWE

PUBLISHING POETRY, LITERATURE, ART,

MUSIC FOR HUMANITY'S SAKE

A BRAND NEW PUBLISHING COMPANY

FOUNDED 2020

SAN FRANCISCO

ISBN: 979-8-9870259-8-7

Library of Congress Control Number : 2023947263

EBOOK ISBN: 979-8-9870259-9-4

Shape this fedora

The brim of our tango noir

Smoke curling over

Shoulder looking at me eyes

Sadly smiling whisper this

For Mercedes

Contents

Destiny Murder

She folded my brain

So much Saturday laundry

The rotating fan in the corner

Pushes its little heart's worth

Of heat from one corner to the other

Still hot sweaty 11 pm

Night

Cracked concrete hard

On my back smoking

Wonder how long the plume lasts

Longer than gunshot last blood spurt

Flip a coin to bet myself

I win

I lose again

Looking up at the ceiling

Apocalypse

DESTINY MURDER!

Empty Hiram's rye bottle on the floor

Ice bucket few drops left of slush

It's roadside motel hot in strangeness

Number 41 this month

I carry a gun

It's a job

It seems like a blink

From before midnight

To first bird chirp

No sleep

No shower

Dress

Coat hat shirt tie

Hangman's noose loose

I am sweaty

It's sweaty

It's a bad bad day

DANE INCE

I head for bad breakfast

In bad coffee shop

It's black and bad stubble

Reflection the coffee steam clears in a moment

I see me in the bottom of my second cup of joe

May the waitress sloshes coffee all day

Putting on my hat

I watch her and wonder

Lighting a cig

See her move through the diner

Looking through windows

I wonder with that body and mind

What she does for fun

There is nothing but shade

Still it is hot

No place at all for coolness

DESTINY MURDER!

On the highway now heading west Route 66

Destiny Murder

Destination Hell

Eternal

In the presence of the eternal

Flower long before bees

Since there is but one

It feels odd to speak of skies

95 million years ago

Ancient

Magnolia

Fossils in the cave walls

People made altars

Prayers for queens, crops, rain, and babies

Died across oceans on the same day

One crowned cold gold and stone jewels

One crowned by the hearts of her children

Her family her youth her hard day's honest work

Light a candle for the queen

There is only one sky

Evergreen

DESTINY MURDER!

Aromatic

Ovate for cooking

Low gray scalloped sky

Will not lift off this humid oppression

Finally this heat wave broke

Too late for you

Altar in the street

Look at the ocean we swim in

Celebration of the life of the queen

The king is bound for prison

For what he done

The children guarded now by strangers

Way too late

For God and country

We failed to do our duty

Now we lay down wreaths

Laurel leaves and magnolia blossoms

DANE INCE

Candy bars

Teddy bears and flowers and flowers and flowers

Washed away on tsunami tears

Wasting for what

Hacked and headless

Turn right on Laurel Street

Your destination is on the left

Magnolia Avenue

Black slatted view fence

Pewter apartments painted tragically

The color bleeds upon gray sidewalk black

We are connected

Roots of trees in the forest

Like that connected

O death

Why do you make me sing

O tragedy why do you make me lament

DESTINY MURDER!

When all I would rather

Is leaves in breeze

We celebrate the life of the queen

The monarch is a ghost in the laundry room

Her children will have a hard time remembering

Above the earth

The house of clouds and rainbows

The overcoat where the sun is hung

Look into its pocket the galaxy of stars

The plural is uncommon

Unlike the number of queens

More than stars

More than the number of flowers

And helium balloon hearts

That mourners leave behind

On the passing of the monarch

Cats slept in September heat

DANE INCE

Do not say skys

Ever when

Skies is the correct form

Lay down this dozen pink roses

Lay down this poem

Lay down these tears

In the stream of life with others

Prayers hung on parchment air

We knew this window would close

We knew it would happen

There will be war

Not there anymore

The call come now

Better hurry

Don't be late

The day the queen died

We are left with things

DESTINY MURDER!

Work in this apple orchard

All undone

Still to do

We must

Printing

Publishing

Specialist supplements in the town of San Carlos

Affix the proclamation's great seal to all our hearts

Our own secret private Scottish oath

On our accession more fully upon the throne of life

Attend the Royal Exchange to proclaim our solidarity

The firing of our will at the tower of hate for women

Give direction that this will end because we proclaim it so

Proclaim this from our hearts and minds

Promise faithfully

DANE INCE

With the whole enduring course of our lives

Guided by New or Old Testament or whatever holy book

Lights your mountain way

Be it psithurism

Wave on beach

Grasshopper

Or prairie dog chatter

Maintain and abide the lovable laws

Love of humanity

Woman

Child

Man

Without exception

Keep justice and equity in your heart

Within this realm as practiced

It should be

Now received

DESTINY MURDER!

This sacrifice now bitter sacrament oppose and abolish

The contrary

The false

The lies of men

All kind of wrong

Some of them call religion

Being all kinds of wrong

Theft

Oppression

In all times coming

Root out all heresy and enemies

Affix the seal and proclamation

Of open soul and flourish

True and perfect

Peace

The horror of death

And violence against love

DANE INCE

Against the best part of humanity

Makes us need to

Faithfully affirm this solemn

Oath

The queen rests in harmony and in heaven

Cup

Where does this thing go

Sharp pieces of broken cup

Here now life's lessons

Inspiration mosaic

Morning writes this form poem

Everything

Can nothing fill me like the everything

Of the answer on your lips

Everything can fill me empty

Staring into the you

The blackness

The universe of brown eyes smile

That black mirror reflects the wreckage of war

Nothing can fill me fuller than the savage attack of butterflies

Nothing can fill me fuller than my standing in front of you

Burnt by the frozen

Offering my bloody heart to you bleeding

In my melting ice cream hands

That scene never made it to the final cut

I cried out to God for salvation and he laughed stabbing

Broken bottle alley taunting

Nothing can fill me

But everything will do

DESTINY MURDER!

Feels

You will be changed after the flood

After the earthquake melted your ice cream cone

After the conflagration

Frozen you so hard

You need an ice pick to answer the phone

You will be changed

The routine will strike

Now like boiling rain

It is like that

That is what I saw

I am a witness

I swear you will never be the same

Flat on my back

On the rooftop flat

Looking skyward

Orange gelato heaven floating horror above

That is what I saw

DANE INCE

My eyes see sadness

What am I doing here

I could be pulling and pushing together

Someplace else

For now I inhabit Strangersville

Alone I weep like everyone who feels

DESTINY MURDER!

Poet's grocery list

Blood oranges

Hearts of palm

Everything in the store that is red

And salt for the wounds

DANE INCE

Examples of suicide notes

I pull off the mask so you may see

The ghoulish torture written upon my face

The horror is such a funny joke

Kids hit by cars

Poison in the candy

Trick or treat

Camus claims Sisyphus is happy

Look at all these fools dancing

Hoping to ward off decrepitude tomorrow

Hoping the haunting will subside

The stinging crying will fall silent

Will fall silent on your deaf hospital ears

Nothing left to hear

But the whisper of the Colt 1911

45 caliber cartridge in your ear

All will be met by harvest

So it is the time to fill our bellies

DESTINY MURDER!

Dance laugh and cheer

Let's get drunk and fuck

You as a cop

Me as a nurse

Oooh officer I have been bad

Broken the law arrest me right now

These high heels are killing me

The costumes will for a moment divert

The terror in our souls

Some welcome the visit of the dead

Momma Papa Granny

Baby Betty Sue

Light their way back to the altar

With candles and lay marigolds along the path

They will be thirsty and hungry from their long journey

Back to the ventana leave them water bread bounty

Bounty of the harvest so they know they left us full of

DANE INCE

Knowledge

And now they can rest in peace

Remember as long as remembered they are living and not

Dead

While others party like Mardi Gras

Till they blow their brains out

To get back at you and cancer

And all the crazy zoo

Let's party like a party

Till we die gruesome large the body count

In drunken highway crash

Go fast

Go fast

Step on the gas

Live even faster still

We need dusty distance between us

And ghosts seeking thrills

DESTINY MURDER!

The devils

The demons

The holy saints who torture and torment

From the day we are stripped screaming from the womb

Till we are worm food wrapped in darkness evermore

DANE INCE

Night clouds

Wake up like it is Sunday

Wake up like it's Sunday

Like it's Sunday morning in an old family photo

But it is Tuesday 3:54 am

Many years after you are dead

You are there daddy with Ted Al and Bob

Only a rectangle for art on the wall

In black white and gray

You already

Getting ready for work

That's in the picture

What you're wearing white shirt

Pressed black pants

Handlebar mustache staring out

Not smiling

In the background on the sofa

Some kind of mystery

DESTINY MURDER!

Stuffed toy

Head and paws down

Fluffy butt up in the air

The stuffed toy has its own fluffy little stuffed toy

Old silk curtains with hems

The secrets we did not know them

We whisper fearfully now

Uncertain

Ephemera

The wake up the wake up on Tuesday it's a Sunday on knees

Praying praying like it's Sunday

The ghost

Visitation

From out of night clouds

My pillow

Lonely

Is holding me down

DANE INCE

Kissing

Under picture book covers

It comes out

Under night clouds

DESTINY MURDER!

What's your favorite way

<u>to celebrate your birthday?</u>

I was in love with a nun

A beautiful wonderful nun

I sinned the biggest and best sin ever with her

I cheated with her on my wife

It was the worst wicked way in the most Hieronymus Bosch

Worst way

The Garden Of Earthly Delights all in a pickle sandwich

She opened me up like a killed rabbit and ripped out the guts

Of my soul

I loved it laughing happy all without taking off my clothes

Junkie jonesing begging more

I had nothing left for home when I returned from that soul

Love fucking

Dry mean and nasty filled with shame sinning

The tragedy the wrecking

You know it is really real when everything is shifted

DANE INCE

When a simple question is torture inquisition

You will do almost anything to fight the urge

To sputter stutter curse how it is

Really seeming now

No one wants to hear

No one wants to hold a bag of smelly bones weeping

Hugging good cheerful smiles

Fading gray distant dying eyes not blinking

You have to tape them closed

If you want them to stay shut

Staples will do too

It doesn't work like it does

In the movies

Why not ask me to balance Martian math

And the answer cannot be any answer

Except a scrillpen exponential to the power schrimp zen

Did she want an answer

DESTINY MURDER!

Or really an answer

It is an innocent enough question

I stumble over every day

Oh that is sweet thanks for asking

I do not have an easy answer

For years it was nonexistent

For years steak and mezcal

And

The next looks like it will be just

Blackness

My favorite way to celebrate was when my

I just can't answer

How should I answer

She is married to the church

She so holy holy holy

I am just a sinner wanting her badly

If I answer I'd be asking

DANE INCE

For her to

For her to fall down sinning the most holy nasty

I am broken now

So I would lie to avoid any further fracture

I could not stand an honest reply

So I am desperate to figure out the best lying lie

Something I can put over easy and smile

She is holy married to the church

And holy God is husband honoring Him her duty

And she has children depending on

Right now I might be happy with a fin

For the track

A shoeshine

And a bottle of gin

But she could send me a happy sunny smiley face

Like daughters send their daddies

That would be crazy and I would have a laugh

DESTINY MURDER!

Hot LA

In Jumbo's Clown Room

The dancing is vacant

Bored chatter

Interesting

Ha

Floating acoustic tile ceiling

Irony in a strip mall

I am here on business

Bad business

Ready for the worst

Rah Rah runs this rub joint

She knows guys who know guys

I am not saying if they are wise or not

It's a job

Out in Bel Air

The walls thick

High

DANE INCE

We need inside

She is good at it

Good at lying

If that isn't what she really does for a living

Then go ask Crow to explain it

That is what he does

It's just a living

Sets everything straight

Keeps the books in pen

Makes no mistakes

If you are crooked does it matter how

How crooked is too crooked too much

Are you crooked just a little

Like a smile

Or are you how now brown cow

Deep and wide like the Hudson

If you lie for a reason

DESTINY MURDER!

If you steal for a reason

A good reason

To make it better

For someone else

Someone in need

Who says what then

So you take something

Something of value out of your father's house

He owed it to you anyway

The old man lied to you and your husband

Stiffed on the wedding gifts

Even when your man did everything asked

The old man hunted you down to Chicago

He searched the place

Came up empty handed

You hid the goods

DANE INCE

Sitting pretty the hiding of the loot

Stand up the old guy says

You blinking

Daddy I'd love to help

But it's my time of the month

Storming out with nothing blankety blank

Slamming doors off the hooks he the old man did

Scramming you and your husband west out to the coast

It was burnt toast the stolen loot left behind

Lost the golden ticket to bliss

After six meekly weak drinks

I can't remember how it ends

Maybe there was a nation built

DESTINY MURDER!

Maybe she built a people

My contact never shows

I stumble out from heat

To hotter than hell

Even when I am drunk I get no relief

Smog summer hot LA

Most days always

DANE INCE

Ugh

I confess to missing

The sound of your voice every day

Even just a word

A sound ah um ugh yes no

With new ears I listen now

Technicolor

We go way back back

Before the war ended

Yeah you follow that

What war when

There is no end

That is why they call it endless war

Wow now I am arguing in my head to myself

I just love rye whiskey water back let's have another

One time I went into a bar

The bartender started to sweat

He saw a bulge in my pants

You got a gun he squeaked

Nah I just keep my wallet in my right front pocket

It's to thwart thieves

I laughed I carry a gun

But my hammer rides in a holster

Never see it coming

DANE INCE

Tap in the tack

Rap rap rap

It's what I do Its my job

Almost have a second career

Waiting to kill time

It's a killing

Ha inside joke

If you were alive then you know what I mean

After the war means something

Anyway

It is a love story

I think of her in tight red lips

Rogue like a costumed character in a costume drama movie

Technicolor

The movie poster in yellow arching letters spitting bullets

Reads Rah Rah McCool is the Whore of Babylon

Just an innkeeper some say

DESTINY MURDER!

You know that thing some people do with cherry stems

Tie them in knots with their tongues

In closed mouths

Rah Rah can do that

But she does it to your mind

Stood up again

I guess

Contact still no show

Still waiting thinking

Your life depends on the tools

Toolbox full of hammers

Hammers are pieces of art

Ball- peen hammer

For metal shaping

Punch hammer to keeps the punches from mushrooming

No one wants a mess all over the place

Rubber mallet no marring quiet

DANE INCE

Claw pound to fit paint to finish

When you want to send a message

Soft blow hammer rawhide wood

Dead blow hammer

Doesn't bounce back

Brass hammers focus the blow precisely on the gear shaft

Bring out the big guns when you need to get things moving

SLEDGE HAMMER

This time a hammer is a gun

Apart

He was a man who carried change in his pocket so that

People would know he had money

She was a woman who made everyone lose their sense of

Direction and drink too much absinthe

They could not dance together

And they were terrible apart

There are letting goes of different types sizes and shapes

Some have color you can taste

I can think of reasons why

But there is sand

Do you feel a sameness in our differences

More crackers for bed

Isolation says all kinds of things

So seduction swish of tail curl up and purr

DANE INCE

Lick

Lick she said

How she got up on my shoulders I don't know

But she did pulled up her cotton summer dress

Well off no panties on now

On my shoulders

With her hairy pussy right in my face

She says lick lick it

Hesitation moment for a moment

The next thing

Grabbing hands full of hair

Yanking

Jerking me hard

My head back

Staring big emerald eyes into my soul

Burning my cornea blind

You slow

I said lick don't stop until you know

Till it's time to stop baby

You will know when

Released my head

Face buried deep

Thick unmown lawn

Jungle lust

Wild I am flush

I am hard

Wafts lavender French milled soap

Smells wet woman

Wet sweet smells

Searched around tongue

Hunting through jungle lush undergrowth

My tongue is shy

In case there are tigers

DANE INCE

Lurking prowling nearby

Preying upon innocent unwary tongues

Swirling around looking

Looking for silkworm

Looking for hard slickworm

She yanked my head back

Again pulled her lips wide apart

Winston Churchill victory sign

Exposing a throbbing beating red hot heartbeat

In front of my face

Glistening wet

See pulse beating in her head

The head of her clit

Lick it now

Lick it now don't stop

Till you know

Released my head again face

DESTINY MURDER!

Now wet with her wet slippery mango juice

I was surprised by the size of her beautiful hot hands

She left murder suspect fingerprints

All over my crime scene face

Traces of her wetness in my hair stick

Evidence of DNA

In case I do not get out alive

Flooding juicy

The ride

Grabbing clawing riding

This big human dick

She slammed into my face

Riding hard

Bucking and fucking my tongue

So hard

I wonder if damage was done

The sound of an ow exhaled like a sigh

DANE INCE

Stopping in mid glide

Yanking Seeing Her handiwork wrought on my red face

Like chocolate and bourbon melting

She swallows the words

Oh is poor baby

Hurt

She is pulling my hair hurting

I nod weakly affirmative

With her grasping and holding

Holding my head just where she want its

All I can do is lick the blood running

Salty down from the split in my lip

Say yes it hurts

She smiled

Saying good good good

Like each good was a different rhyming word

Good she directed me back to the slide

DESTINY MURDER!

Back to the work

Licking long wide

Licking

Everywhere a slick chevron should be licked

Hands full of the hair on my head

My mane

She guides galloping

I lick up and down up and down

Searching memorize the feeling

Up and down up and down

The hardening harder squeezing squeezing

The releasing

The squeezing gliding

The hard dart growing harder keep licking licking

Lick it the swivel of hip I feel her hard bones under soft skin

Hips thrusting and thrusting and thrusting

Up and down on my tongue

DANE INCE

My tongue caught between her clit and a hard place

My lip and front teeth

Slowly I crumble to the ground

She does not lose her place

She does not lose her rhythm

Not a single missing stoking stroking beat

Clit on my tongue

Flicking clit on my tongue

Clit on my tongue

Her clit glitter on my tongue

Don't stop keep going

Keep licking keep going keep going

Keep going keep going keep going

She is fucking my face the gallop to win

To finish just like she likes it

To finish the squeeze release

And

DESTINY MURDER!

Finally relax to collapse

Just the way she wants it.

Glitters

The voice in my head said

The rain will not come

Godlike whisper says other

Morning

I do not listen

I say it will

When we finish

Lying next to each other

Romance the light bends

Back the slice of night's prism

Heals this insanity

Welds this division

You float me off

The hold us close

I love to watch your finger dance

Your full lips fuck my mind into

The rhyme and rhythm of simple gibberish

DESTINY MURDER!

And kiss

The slightly opened mouth twist

The tug and plug of flicks

Smiling pieces fit

The breath

You know what you are doing to me

That sly smile says so

I do it back

The dazzle flow

At the end we each acknowledge

Glow appreciations thank yous holy and soft strokes

The sleepy sexy eyes hold all

That glitters

And love's laugh

The ocean in the teardrop's dream

We drive on both sides of the road

The thunderclap storming

DANE INCE

Wonder of the thighs

Our manes tango tangle

Tapping smooth

The lovers statue falling

Melting chocolate in our hands hiding

Licking palms

Clasping on the gallop

The poem finished too

And into a reverent dream we are making

DESTINY MURDER!

Bookstore

Found in a Venice Beach used book store

"N.E. Will Not Be Silent" Porridge Press 1980

An except-

From "Fucking in the Disney Land Hotel"

In Anaheim, California 1957

Nowita Edgcliff and Patty Siparia

Take Disneyland by storm

Nowita is the most famous unknown beat poet

She is in a couple with Patty

Pretty Patty goes by the pen name Vamp Poison

A Cheltenham poet known for her titles like

"Bondage- A Lesson in Love"

"Tender Tears- Love is Misery, Cry Mercy"

Hats with veils

Heels

Gloves

Seamed stockings perfect straight

DANE INCE

Technicolor red lips suck on cigarettes

Waiting on the platform

For the shiny hard phallic monorail train

To slide smoothly into the hotel station

Imagine Grace Kelly and Vivien Leigh

Smoking on the platform

Cancer smoke curling over shoulders

Then you appreciate the smolder

Of the adventure soon to ensue

Tomorrowland will never be the same

The couple soon learns this is no place

If you are thirsty for a martini

They swagger and look

Look at everything

They look at each other

With that looking look lovers know

The invitation for

DESTINY MURDER!

Middive

Morning drunks were never very entertaining

They have the purpose of oblivion

Every poem is a death poem

The black cat sits in midnight dark

Casting a long shadow

Trips me into middive

Police lineup

You drift to deepness

I am left here alone

It is just perception

Of blanket gone missing in the night

The kicked off calamity now sleeping on the floor

This is how to play the game of life

I ride the torus

The spiral escalator returns me to future past

I dreamed the tattoo on your shoulder came to life

Killed me November

5:54 pm dark

Alone the clotted stain

The coroner's report

A scribble

I cannot decipher what it means

The invitation to shower with

Withdrawn

DESTINY MURDER!

I worry this new lover

Will fall in love with that old lover

My terror house is papered in torment

Green and pink floral pattern

A prison bar motif

I see every wrinkle written on my soul

Across the bay the roses

Rose garden waiting for my visit

40 years ago

I sit frozen in my mess

Old and a wreck

Soon to be toothless

Forgotten

Locked in a chest

Irrelevant

The smell of musk

And rainbows taunts

DANE INCE

Nothing may be described

Maybe

Mind-blowing

How not to finger someone

2 for the pink and one for the stink

Have you ever been in a police lineup

Blinding hot lights

Saying what cannot be said

I hear your breath change

Fire alarm warning

Somewhere there is happiness

Like cats sleeping

Midnight

Go lobby gee

Thousand Oaks

Luxury

Are you calling Mr. Franco

Talking to the neighbor's dog

Who's a good boy

And now for the butter sauce

This pulse

This scene

Imagine the flight

The sad night

Your last slipped through fingers

The oyster knife stab

Chicken neck crab bait

Wrestle the shape of beasts

The slice of night from sunset

The mountain chair

DANE INCE

The collection of everything

This whipping post

The airline stewardess

Messed up hair

Rouge lipstick for cheek rouge

Retold the saga

Like Gabriel raised a bent finger to Mohammed

Said go that way

In a cave

In a dream

In between

That million year heartbeat

Frozen tear

Is that datura snow

I dream of you coming home

Can you call it that that that

I have clothes to wear

DESTINY MURDER!

Suitable suits to scare spirits souls right out of here

I feel like climbing up

Riding this horse again

Dog follows

Dog bothers

Bareback

No bridle just the mane

I fly off on the gallop

The dog licks my face

That's what happened to me

Midnight

Upon time

DANE INCE

They

They lie to you

The they that always is the they

I have my reporter's pad and recorder

I am counting the dead

Writing down numbers

The memory now seems lined paper thin

Just a moment ago we were pulsing in bed

What was said I can't remember

Smiles faded newspaper photo on a pile and piles

Of undone things unfinished

The varnish can open

Now gelatin pickle

No sparkle twinkles in unsmiling eyes

Waiting for dead papa to walk them down the aisle

Since you are dead 4 times broken

Smashed to bits

Diamond dust

DESTINY MURDER!

Collects on wrists and hands

I know I will have to take it one more time and again

And again

This is correspondence from the war

This is how we send wreckage gifts

Wrapped in Halloween masks

Turkey gravy

Eight candles flicker lit

I read the notes from coffee stained pad

I wonder what for I show you every single scar

What good will it do

From behind this old brick wall I am sobbing

Even I cannot

Cannot

Listen to the screaming in my soul

Weary sometimes I cannot lift my head

Up and off this angry

DANE INCE

Hot pillow with its licking tongue dreams

Trying to seduce me

One more time

Into hate sex with myself

The pickup line heard before

Now works every fucking time

On my broken knees I offer the treasure of wounds blood

And pus

Head down smiling like this is all that is left but it is really

Rubies, gold and diamonds

And

Secret children's dreams of joy

Here take this plate of entrails

Build us a country cottage fine

Riot of flowers in the garden

Where butterflies dance

Just silly clowns

DESTINY MURDER!

I am sorry

I am not ready yet

I still have to ferment

I take back the offer

Put those guts back in the cupboard

The maggots not yet fully grown

When they have flown away adults

I will look and go see again

The prognosis may still be poor

Poor is still better than the ending never

Never never

Tomorrow I will fill a new notebook

Full with tragedy joy and wonder

Ponder ever and ever the still wanting heart

Morning sunlight sneaking through the slices in the blinds

DANE INCE

Life takes you if you let it

To streams pools understanding of the words in the myth

The cartouche on tomb wall easily readable like the National

Inquirer's story of "Ratboy from Mars"

Inner outer

I hope to see the amber altar

The way the blind kiss it with fingers

The shine of sun through window

Ghosts residing nearby

The spirit of the host

Guides

The home of the resting crystal

After you talk I cannot stop crying

I was ashamed of what I had done

Asking for the largest slice of pie

You sliced a piece of your heart put it on a plate

Smiling human grace

I hope I was not selfish

But I was

Really

It was not a heart part you cut out

But bloody cancer poison

DANE INCE

A zombie spore infection

That crippled angel wings

Limp and failed to kill you

I see only a little of what you have been through

Fly like arrows stabbing

Wounds

The final beheading

Making martyr of you you saint

You smile when you step off out

But I saw you like you were before

When you were in prison praying

Lashed with stones and thrown into the lake

Tortured and tormented

Still you would not break

Still you were true

A week in the furnace

The flame not burning the song and spirit of you

DESTINY MURDER!

You find a way to come as fully free yourself

Right

On

Through

They boiled your tongue in the soup

You spit blood in their face

They were blinded and still persisted

Never knowing when they had had enough

They tried to ruin the sailing ship of your body

Chopping down your masts

Cutting out what they thought made you defiant woman

And still they did not learn

That you are in the image of

And no mortal kills Ggod

Before I knew how you were then

I felt so honored

In a holy way

DANE INCE

You sleep on dirty shirts on the floor

You see what I love here

It is you here and the constellation

You bring

The constellation here of my own

I love it here

Here I am

Trunk of desperation tricks

Pity is a currency of negative value

The hole is there holy

I do not even cry about it anymore

I do not know how to be

I do not know what to do

DESTINY MURDER!

Everyone is more than me

The me of nothing

I gave away all the midway tickets

Now I am stupid

Even adolescent memory

Just terrorize me

I know even though

The excuse

I wobble off into inner outer space

DANE INCE

Pebbles

I throw Pebbles down

Down a silent dark deep well

Hoping for an echo

Blue sky distant splashing sound

Leave this here now in the wind

Bongo

Hey bongo player

Bongo

Bongo me an intro

Bongo me a bridge

I fill in the sorry words

Snap the happy sadness

You beat on the skins

Bongo Bongo Bongo

Till yeah yeah the end

I want to see this drive-in picture

One more time

Again again

Bongo till the beginning

Bongo

DANE INCE

For sure

I am on diet so I won't die

After surgery

That is all that is allowed

Because everything I need to survive

In my guts

Has been killed

They want to see if the flora will come back

So

They give me more pills

The mortician is laying the odds

Taking the bets

Man walking alive

Or dead

The executioner knows

The phone lines are cut

There will be no reprieve

None that can be coming

DESTINY MURDER!

My humor assassinated

Now I read every poem on dead death and dying

As the funniest thing

Since Thurber or Samantha Bee

A tsunami washed over my papier mâché heart

Dripping and oozing

What is left is the muck in my hands

How long will it hold together

Just gluey pieces of pus

My Annabel Lee I am mourning

How long will kind words from afar

Hold the surgical staples in place

I ghost without them for sure

DANE INCE

Hot September

I sit here in hot September

A mere drop in the ocean

Putting pen to page

Because you died

I cry

Alone

I know there is someone who knows the price of admission

But she lives only in my dreams

Because she is an angel, I have cooked up

She can never kiss me

Like I think my mortal flesh needs

She is what everyone wants that missing thing you cannot do

for you

She misses that too

She brings that other touching

Saying yes I am here in hell with you

The peeling off of flesh can last for years and years

DESTINY MURDER!

Till San Joaquin river summer dry is tearless

Nothing left to cry

There is a ferry leaving every second

To cross the river Styx

Ever coming back never

I would trade you

To be young and stupid

Not to have more life in front of me

But for salvation from the understanding of what words
Really mean

DANE INCE

Lonely Hearts Killers

From 1946 to 1949

A Merchant Marine who was a brilliant British spy

Called Raymond Martinez Fernandez

To be known later as RMF

Got conked in the head a wonder not to be dead

Fractured his skull

Brain parts were damaged

Lost control of social and sexual behavior

Then did a brief stint in the pen

A school for black magic and conversion to Voodoo

His personal Zen led him to answer a Lonely Hearts personal

ad

Where he met his honey Martha Jule Beck

Later we know her as MJB

A "glandular problem" to explain her weight

Premature puberty promiscuous

MJB was raped by her brother

DESTINY MURDER!

Beat by her mother for the trouble of sin

She buried her sorrow in fantasy magazines

The throb of romantic novels

And Lonely Hearts personal ads

That is where MJB fell under the spell of RMF

His charm and irresistible power

They made a plan

Lured Lonely Hearts personal ad responders

Helped them to get dead

Their isolation was hammers to heads

RMF and MJB were so kind to end

To end the misery of the miserable loneliness

With a choking, a strangle and drowning

Now if the Lonely Heart were merely depressed

They fixed that easy

DANE INCE

With a shot to the head

You should be locked up and hiding

Fearing the dread

These rascals rampage even now

Isolation loneliness and depression

Are not just in your head

These are not New Lonely Hearts Killers

Not in the least

Been around forever

And still on the spree

Launching a new crimewave

They are shooting and stabbing all over the place

Killing unaware folks dead

Haven't you heard it's headline news

Isolation loneliness depression are doing us in

DESTINY MURDER!

Not just a mental problem alone just in the head

Better call the cavalry

An expert or a friend

Call some lonely person you may know

Who you can defend

Good for them

Good for you

Shelter in place is alarming

Causes a significant increase

In the risk of premature dying

Not just the vapors but misery

These killers are real as the experts say

What, what, my amygdala is shrinking

My heart is attacking

My blood pressure increasing

Better make a routine

Stick to it

It matters the day

And that you can say it

Get a plan for connection

Call Momma

Call Daddy

Call those that you love and know

To just say hey how's it going

You okay

Pets can keep up immunity

And are just fun to snuggle

Stand up and fight

So you won't be a victim

Of poor sleep. impairment

DESTINY MURDER!

Cognitive decline

You are too beautiful

I would be sad for you

To be just one of the numbers

A victim of the Lonely Hearts Killers

Because this never happened

<u>this is not a Costa Rican Beach</u>

In one story they are poets

In another gangsters on the lam

And in another they argue if God

Is a man

Is a woman

There can be no denial

That the fabric is woven

Drapes across the box

Oh God oh God

If you have lived

You are lucky

Or maybe not

You know the lamentation

The ecstatic exaltation

Oh God oh God

Lying here now

In this state

Subsiding tumescence

I feel her watching

Guiding all along

Not a single word written that was not written out before

Newspaper ink

Half-tone photo front page plane crash

The couple walks on the beach

Sunglasses

Shirts unbuttoned flapping

Surfer shorts and sand

She watches all

Some believe it is arrogant to attempt to be above God

Perfectly finishing all their work

DANE INCE

They leave a brick or two without any mortar

As if God was worried or cared about mortal arrogance

Across the rich coast she sees

The hangman

The noose

The improbable love of gangsters

The love across time

She sees what she has written

She finishes her drink

She is every character

She is no character at all

She is none of them

She is all of them

She is the writer

The suture sewing up this wound

DESTINY MURDER!

The beach sand that sticks to the soles of dead men's feet

Shuffling in summer heat humid

Dead in their dream

The question

The answer

There is always more

The men strolling on the beach

Stop

Pull out handguns

Shoot the ocean waves

All their ammo spent

They are done

They are alone in paradise

Happy

They laugh about the money

DANE INCE

For their hit job well finished

They are drunk

The hurricane is coming

Watching from the cabana

Shaded by palms

How the story ends is known

With that stumbly afternoon buzz

Notebook grabbed up

Pencils erasers and nubs too

The newspaper revealed upon the table

The photo

Two Poets Dead

Fiery plane crash

Off the coast

Ah the list is so long now

DESTINY MURDER!

We forget more than we could ever know

Two poets dead

The hurricane is coming coming coming

DANE INCE

How to

How to paint a poem with a toothpick

Canker sore

Prime the linen canvas

With vacant looking

Future smile

I wonder where you went then

Crumble down to granite curb

The propaganda

The deed

The theory

The violin high note I am bowing

Muddy Waters growls

How to paint a sunset

With nothing but question marks

How to paint an oaky knot

Losing is all that

Solitary window sash

DESTINY MURDER!

And what is the use to

How to paint a tree

I explained all that to you in Waco

In summer when wisdom took its tool

Carved the leather indentations

In my latest dream

The one I remember

The piles of cherry pits

Something good must have gone on

Like an Emma Goldman lullaby

The burning yahrzeit candle

Last December

Soon I will light another

When will I be finished

I know now never

Luba made me an honorary member of the tribe

Gertie the 4'11" bail bondsman rides

DANE INCE

In the front seat

Shotgun shogun

She is strapped with a pearl-handled pistol

Always carries but she has no need

Nothing hurts her heart of steel

The melon seeds fly

She spits bullets

How to paint kitchen cabinets

How to paint a lie

How to paint a room

How to paint clouds

The magic drifts by

See the panther crouching

At the bottom of Jacob's ladder

How to how to

How to find the words

How to be okay

DESTINY MURDER!

How to paint a wall

Surrounding safe

How to paint a way out of here

Leaving no clues at all

How to paint metal

How to paint furniture

How to paint a house to play house in

When the parents are all dead

Old enough to know better

Young enough to do it anyway

How to paint a car

How to paint IKEA furniture

How to paint with acrylics

How to paint with blood

How to paint with bony fingertips

Naked in the mud

How to paint marble for real

With watercolor tears

How to

An excuse for more beer

Perfect never wrong

Listen to the song

DESTINY MURDER!

Rouge

I dip a finger into the hole in my chest

This blood of blood

With this pool

I rouge my lips

My lonely lips

Gray to bloody red for kissing

Puckered red and ready waiting

Dumbly wonder why

No lover's attraction coming

No pollen for this addiction

This is all of me on me only about me

I hesitate to shape the words and say a thing

I watch the fountain drain

The memory

The brief comma

I disdain

The black cloud

DANE INCE

That blocks the sun

Refusing to rain

When all the ache

Wants is for the rain to bleed

It is just a tickle

No it is just a pain

Insane ignitions fail

Shiver works

The blows

The blows

The blossoms wrinkled closed

I wait for the blink

Seeing none I sleep

I dream and dream

The future terrors

I cannot speak

This burden is mine

DESTINY MURDER!

Mine to carry

Bandage to carry for a wound

Diamonds are less than perfect

For their inclusions include

Sometimes other diamonds within their insides deep

Their sparkle seems shining less

For the occlusion

I stick my fingers down my throat

Straighten my swollen tongue

I breathe I breathe

I smile warm under blankets

Dream of spring through trees

Cold air moves under

Heavy weighed down

The mass under mass

DANE INCE

Warm air lighter laughing rises

Shies away fluffy dancing

Weather

This is passing too

DESTINY MURDER!

Riven

Sometimes there is no way out

It is a sweaty corner

It is bad

I am stupid

But I am here

Tap dance like crazy without moving a muscle

You face death

It's a job

Steel revolver pointed right at you

A moment of clarity

Sweat rolling down your face is alarming

Mistaken as a sudden move to the loom of your death

They fear the lift

They fear for their life

Here in the galvanized steel Quonset warehouse baking

Desert heat

In that fraction of time

DANE INCE

Grinning thinking calmly of dancing pandas

With smile and charm I assure assailant

That there are no worries

It is all a mistake

They show up

I show up

All according to plan

But not did

Done a damn thing done like it was supposed to be done

Did they

Now everyone is here empty handed

Except for hands full of guns

Black falling darkness

Face down on the concrete the kiss of hardness

The only thing that is color cool

Riven with lead

The red lake is flowing sleepy and smooth

DESTINY MURDER!

My eyes closing on the scene of you

Folding fresh white sheets from the clothesline in the

Backyard

My brain unfolding the folds

It is a long dolly shot that ends with a rack focus kind of day

The end

About the author

The awakening began in a small grove of black oak trees on Collins Street in Fort Worth, Texas. Then the road wound around a few stops in other towns and cities of Texas, Zapata, Del Rio, and finally ending with radio days in Space City. Under summer fog and the strong lure of Berkeley, Dane Ince came west to study fine art and acting and to write ever so occasionally. Personal tragedy and the pandemic focused the artist's mind and hundreds of poems have resulted along with special online programing events on Facebook, the most recent event being a poetic gathering of writers from around the world in support of Ukraine. Dane Ince is an internationally published poet, hosts a weekly open mic "Time to Arrive", Beat Poet Laureate for California 2022-2024, and publisher at EYEPUBLISHEWE.COM. His first collection of poetry was published in October 2022 titled "The Whole Existential Novel; the journey from the Darkside of the Rainbow to Satchidananda"

About **EYEPUBLISHEWE**

Eye publish ewe (EYEPUBLISHEWE) is a brand new publishing company, founded in San Francisco. Art, music, video, poetry, and other literature will find inclusive shelter here. Quality work produced by the artists' hearts, minds, and souls rather than commercial interests will have this as a home. All are welcomed with open minds and hearts and eyes to the future. Together we will publish art for humanity's sake.

EPE titles

Where Grasses Bend: Poems from Portland to Steens Mountain in the Time of Plagues by **Mimi German** ISBN: 979-8-9870259-5-6

The Green Notebook: Poems on Family, Relationships, Spirituality, Self-Enquiry, Recovery, ACA, Disruption, Death, Walking Through the Mirror, and Cats by **John Angell Grant** ISBN: 979-8-9870259-6-3

The Whole Existential Novel: The Journey from the Dark Side of the Rainbow to Satchidananda by **Dane Ince** ISBN: 979-8-9870259-0-1

Good Grief...Please!: A Dialogue with Death and Life by **Tish Ince** ISBN: 979-8-9870259-2-5

EPE titles

coming soon

A House without Walls: Existential Journeys and Love Poems to Mexico by **Lesley Constable**

"Naturalzela del Amor" poems in Spanish and English by **Martin Del Toro Gutierrez**

www.ingramcontent.com/pod-product-compliance
Lightning Source LLC
Chambersburg PA
CBHW020047310726

48970CB00007B/2444